BlackAmber Books

All that Bl

by the same author

Ma, novel

BlackAmber Books 2002

All that Blue

Gaston-Paul Effa

Translated by
Anne-Marie Glasheen

BlackAmber Books

Published by BlackAmber Books Limited
PO Box 10812, London SW7 4ZG

1 3 5 7 9 10 8 6 4 2

Originally published in France in 1996
under the title *Tout ce bleu* by Bernard Grasset

First published in Great Britain in 2002 by
BlackAmber Books Limited

This book is supported by
the French Ministry for Foreign Affairs,
as part of the Burgess programme administered for
the French Embassy in London
by the Institut Français du Royaume-Uni.

This book is supported by
the French Ministry of Culture
(Centre National du Livre).

A CIP record for this book is available from the British Library

Designed and typeset by Peter and Alison Guy
Printed in Finland by WS Bookwell

ISBN 1–901969–08–8

THE
ARTS
COUNCIL
OF ENGLAND

The Swan

I think of the Negress, gaunt and consumptive,
Trudging through mud, eyes wild, in search of
Glorious Africa's absent coconut palms
Behind a vast wall of fog;

Of those who have lost what cannot be found
Never, never! Of those who drink tears
And suckle Pain like a good she-wolf.
Of the scrawny orphans wilting like flowers …

Charles Baudelaire *(Le cygne)*
Trans. Anne-Marie Glasheen

Douala

Douo was four, maybe five, when his mother was taken from him. In the space of a spasm and without emotion – as though the entrusting of his first-born to the missionaries of the Holy Spirit had encouraged him to turn away from idols and embrace the God of redemption – Douo's father, seated amid the shaggy branches of the mangroves, communicated the troublesome secret to his wife that he had decided to hand his eldest child over to the nuns.

Speechless with grief, Douo's mother clasped her son to her. Her lips exploded achingly into life again and again over the child's body, while her hands, she felt, were discovering him for the first time. She fancied she and Douo had but one pair of shoulders, one and the same pair of hips, that the child had not yet left her womb and that she could keep him encrypted in there. The young mother let out a shriek and clutched the child so tight they were but one flesh.

Her parents had married her to he whom she had been promised at birth but never met. She had followed her husband to a foreign town, far from her nearest and dearest, to a region whose language she didn't know. She was homesick, afflicted by grief and the inability to express herself. She was fifteen years old.

And now, they were taking her child, the only living person with whom she could commune to the limits of feeling. Inside his forehead, his cheeks, his eyes, Douo could feel the contractions of his mother's face. Joined as they were, mother and child reeled. Douo knew the memories he had collected so far were but crumbs, odds and ends, inconsequential scraps compared to this momentous event. Engulfed by this indissoluble bond, Douo would make desperate attempts to sustain what had been truncated before sinking into an oblivion peppered with images from an unreliable and patched-up memory.

Douo was born in the blue shade of a solitary sisal tree. This leafy umbrella, reaching upwards to the sky where clouds of butterflies traced symbols that vanished before they had even been seen, formed a roof of light over the woman giving birth.

Moaning, she laboured alone bent over the child being born. When she saw him emerge, all pink and plump like the heart of a watermelon, she was alarmed to see the mischievous grimace, like a roughly hewn inhuman smile, the many puckers created. And that was how he came into the world, already ashamed of his face. He didn't cry. The first thing he did was throw himself at his mother's breast. Having cut the cord that joined him to her, the mother gazed at the child and chewed at her fingers with pleasure.

▼

When he was born, his mother was fifteen, his father thirty-two. Born young and old, only the light that crisscrossed the memory of his mother was able to repair the tragedy of his double birth. The shadow of his father retreated into an edifice of cruelty. Let the wind sweep away these images frozen in regret and nostalgia, let it gather up his early years to the sacrifice – after all, tradition demanded that the family make a gift to God of the eldest child – that had made a dark pact with his childhood.

At the age of five, he was offered to God by his father, a miracle of indifference, to a little-known divinity, with a detachment, a contempt that made the little boy believe he had never been wanted. Nowhere was family unity more venerated than here, yet nowhere was it so easy to detach yourself from a child you had just brought into the world to entrust him to a God in Whom it had been so difficult to believe.

Was Douo nothing but an offering

to be placed at the foot of an altar? With the absence of his mother his eyes lost their lustre: over his cradle hung the image of a dark humanity that perpetuated crime by using the innocent as fodder. He felt the shudder imprinted in his very flesh from which anguish escaped and then renewed itself.

They waited until Douo was five to circumcise him. The sword of their eyes sliced his flesh. Not allowed to cry, the crimson-faced child saw stars. The moon had bewitched them. And his grief-stricken mother, head in hands, wept in the twilight.

Next day the Sisters of the Holy Spirit came to fetch him. Even though he was being treated like a prince he didn't want to be tended. Again his courage failed him, he found the mere sight of the nuns distressing. When there was nowhere left to run, when it was time to give himself up, he went off on his own, began to undress and waited to be punished. It wasn't so much that he wanted to conceal his thinness but to tremble alone and without shame. He took off his clothes, one by one, and folded them on the grass.

The Sisters were making their way towards him; there was no time to hide. Flustered, he tried in vain to pull in his stomach but the nuns were happy just to plaster his wound with permanganate. They couldn't take their fascinated eyes off the object of their care. They tended it as though it were a small miracle.

▼

He felt both excited and bewildered as he entered the convent. His heartache was not the result of grief, or if it was he wasn't aware of it, but of the sight of his mother's face there in front of him, retreating as he advanced. So near, yet already out of reach.

Images too, for which he could find no explanation, haunted him. The first one returned day after day, like an image from a dream: two large hands raised between heaven and earth. It was the same measured and repeated gesture with which his mother hoisted him onto her back, where he'd stay for days on end watching her hair as it swayed, threatening to collapse, eventually to become integrated with the glorious memory he kept of her.

Already it seemed to him he had nothing in the world but his past, the memories of his early childhood, the blissful sensation of his mother rubbing his body with palm oil. At the thought of this he almost staggered, so excruciating was the wrench in his heart.

What had secretly governed his life since early childhood – the interrupted relationship with his mother – came to him, later, in a flash. The memories were always there and could come flooding back at any time, appearing unexpectedly in the middle of a conversation to distort or obliterate reality and prevent him from seeing anything else. It was as though they were fixed to the nuns' faces, which he'd see as deformed, averted or even transformed.

Douo wondered which of all those women was his mother. Weren't they all his mothers, since none withheld her affection? Why then did they insist on being addressed as 'Sister'? Were they really sisters or were they called sisters to avoid being mothers? For Mother Superior he felt nothing but devotion. Was it her wimple that made her superior to the others? But why couldn't the sisters be someone's mother?

In a silence not unlike the ancient terrors left undispelled by motherhood, Douo had had little experience of a mother's love. In the exhilaration that left the child proud and speechless, he had, unbeknownst to him, renounced intimacy. Was all affection, the moment it was seen as devotion, not in danger of becoming one with its own passion, doomed to a confusing of all values?

For a long time the rustlings of the convent left him wide-eyed with astonishment and bewildered by an abandonment for which childhood had ill prepared him. What kept him going was the hope that, as on the morning of the Resurrection, he would be enlightened by his mother's absence.

The child without a family was, in spite of everything, a child-king. Whenever a tooth had to come out the nuns would make a fuss of him; even Mother Superior, she who, always clutching her rosary, was considered authoritarian. He was plagued and tormented by these both blissful and fascinating images that stabbed at his heart like a knife.

Once memory's dusty cover had been removed, how could he protect himself from such questionable secrets? Was it he, Douo, or another who had actually never stopped being there inside him, who sensed that behind the promise of resurrection there lurked the certainty of deception? It struck him – or had he just invented it? – that it was something quite different, that it was a bewildered, bewildering faith, into which his soul had unwittingly been sucked and where desire eventually wearied and died.

He told himself that the substitute eternity had gone on for too long, that from the luminous crack had come one single unbearable regret. There was what would never come to light, what would forever remain hidden, that motherless faith, flagellated, broken, lying in the mud, with all its wounds, its open sores, with no hope of resurrection, that faith in whose shadow, unconsoled, he would drink dust.

▼

Douo had always had more than one face. Three times he had lost his name. The first was when his mother held him in her arms and whispered, 'Douoooo.' The second was when he left his family to be reborn in the West. The third was when a teacher nicknamed him Papus, since which time, he had known the exquisite pleasure of being none other than the ghost of the last mathematician of the School of Alexandria.

Like the child, gawping at the brightness of a dead star, he took his place amongst the more illustrious dead, with memory that returns like an abandoned forgotten corpse. It was then that memory touched him with its wings; he learned that language was the perfect place to hide one's childhood treasures, to put a name to the face of the dead; the only place where they stood a chance of being invisible and saved.

Sometimes, without actually being conscious of an error or a difference, Douo-Papus felt guilty. A prisoner, he roamed the bewildering opacity he was staring at, which he would have liked to shatter or light up, but which he felt eluded him, for the moment he tried to capture it, it intensified. The cause wasn't difficult to find; his name, or rather nickname – that of a stranger, a white man – had left him forever unworthy of his tribe.

In his eyes, he was nothing but a vague shadow or, worse, a nameless, faceless emptiness. Groping at the fringes of night, he waited to appear to himself before momentous and over-due revelations let loose another figure inside him, a different one maybe from the one he was expecting.

Lifter of his own mask, the one he had chosen – or, that had been chosen for him – he discovered he was black on the outside and white inside, that he was the coconut whose tree grew forgetful of its roots, skinned alive by himself, moving forward, blind like the barn owl.

Squeezing his buttocks tight, Douo-Papus trembled in the night. So great was the darkness he could see nothing. An owl hooting cheered him. Jackals and hyenas lay in wait ready to pounce on him. 'Shall I or shan't I?' wondered Douo-Papus, even though it was a bit late. To avoid an accident two precautions were better than one. He was trying to summon some courage. No bright moon to cheer him and no going back. All he could do was make a dash for the nearest clump of trees to relieve himself.

At an age when children begin to experience emotions in their sleep, Douo-Papus was still wetting his bed. One night, he dreamed he was stretched out in a plane. He opened the window and with a great sense of relief, urinated long into space. The dampness of the sheets dragged him from his pleasure. He woke up.

Innocent, asleep, he had soiled the bed. A long stream was making its way to the corridor. He quickly stripped off the sheet, washed it and hid the offending article. Then he went in search of a fresh sheet, which is why the Sisters always found him clean. Having had more than one accident, Douo-Papus was careful to take precautions. Every night, afraid he would end up having to clean up after himself, that he would have to brave the long dark corridors and the huge cupboards with their creaking doors, he stopped sleeping in his bed and slept on the floor. The perfect coenobite, he could tolerate the tropical cool. When he got up, his bed was already made. The Sisters held him up as an example to the others.

When he didn't make it in time, Douo-Papus would find ways to console himself. 'It was lucky I gave in straightaway; that way my body heat will dry the mat before daybreak.' Relieved, he'd shut his eyes and go back to sleep. The Sisters of the Holy Spirit never understood why he would not join them on their outings. 'Always got his nose in a book, that one,' they'd say. How ashamed he would have felt had they found him dirty! He even had the idea one day of tying an elastic band or shoelace around his penis to avoid enuresis.

The day Douo-Papus was told he was leaving for France he stopped wetting the bed. He still had strange dreams; at the roadside where a milestone was waiting for him as he went to relieve himself; on the riverbank where he pissed profusely.

▼

In his role as the Sisters' son there were no favours to be had. On the contrary, he was often the scapegoat. Whenever the meal wasn't to the boarders' liking, they'd threaten to lock him in the refectory and make him sniff it up. To punish him, they'd pick him to be the reader. Condemned to watching others eat, Douo-Papus carefully selected the more obscure passages from Saint-Exupéry, Simone Weil and Georges Bernanos. At the end of the meal, one of the boarders would taunt, 'There's no meat left. But it doesn't matter, hardboiled eggs are better for intellectuals.'

It was different with the Sisters. At table, wine loosened Father Gaspard's tongue. His hairy, bearded Semitic profile, aquiline nose and cheeks stood out against the dark and he looked like a patriarch in a gothic stained-glass window. Enthusiasm screwed up his eyes and moved his lips over yellowish stumps. He never stopped talking of his time as a legionnaire. His long decrepit body would sway in time to his booming laugh, noisy hiccups would choke him, then he'd hiss between what was left of his teeth, '*Tantum ergo sacramentum* ...'

Suddenly his one good eye, glued to the clammy globe of his monocle, would focus on the Sisters' son, 'Another drop, my son.'

The child, whose colour prevented him from blushing, would turn as pale as the angel of the Apocalypse. As the last button of the Father's filthy cassock burst, an eternal smile froze on the incredulous Sisters' faces. Most were deaf or pretended to be.

Having mixed wine with soup or was it soup with wine, bent over their perpetual broth, they found it difficult to suppress their burps. Douo-Papus wondered how they mixed the two. But then white people did such strange things: only yesterday the Sisters put water in the wine and fresh herbs in the salad. But Douo-Papus was happy, he was at last talking man to man. Like an old soldier, he knocked back the drop

of wine the Father had drowned for
him.

▼

Having no toys, Douo-Papus played at catching flies. The game consisted of catching the insect and holding it in his hand without suffocating it. Buzzing wildly, the fly would tickle his palm as it struggled. It didn't want to die. But Douo-Papus must not give in; he had to be patient, to wait for it to surrender. There would be a final drone from the prisoner then it would fall silent. Was it dead, dying, unconscious or just submissive? As the fly mustered the last of its strength to escape he would pounce. Like one possessed with a rage to get it over and done with, he'd tear off the wings. 'It's a hard life,' he'd say, pinning it up next to his other trophies.

It was Douo-Papus's habit to look after the chicken coop and collect the eggs. All day long he waited for the jubilant cry of a chicken that had just laid an egg. Since his friends didn't lay quickly enough for him, he'd try to encourage them. He'd sit beside them in the grass and cackle in unison with them. The hens scratched tirelessly at the food but wouldn't start laying.

One day Douo-Papus noticed that when the cockerel strutted around with his feathers all puffed out and covered the hen, an egg appeared. So he tethered the hens and encouraged the cockerel. He'd changed sides.

He liked to watch the ducks waddle around the poultry-yard. He'd follow hot on their heels, imitating their hobble, the way they wiggled as they contorted their necks. Had he been able, he would have loved to join them splashing about in the duck pond. But he preferred to keep his distance. He didn't trust them. They might have been tempted, like in the fairy tale, to change into serpents in the night. Douo-Papus studied them, mesmerised by their corkscrew penises that forever trailed in the dust. He loved trampling the wild grass, splashing himself with cold water. He was happy. The sky was clear. It was the joy of the thrill it gave him. Like the child in *L'Enfant*, the first volume of the auto-

biographical trilogy by Jules Vallès, he
thought of becoming a farmer.

▼

The reputation of the Libermann School, founded by the missionaries, was legendary. Old-fashioned and formal, it educated the country's elite. Every morning, as the flag was raised, the pupils sang the *Marseillaise*.

They wore grey, the colour best suited to blend with the dust. Because black children got through so many clothes, the school supplied the uniforms. Rough games were not allowed; barefoot but squeezed into their Terylene suits, they suffocated, wearied by the sun. Douo-Papus would prance around in his crumpled uniform. He and his friends were taught to honour the language of Molière: '*Allons enfants de la martyre, le jour des Noirs est animé* [1].' The Superiors thought it was lovely to hear them singing in their own language!

Douo-Papus couldn't wait for the

[1] Translator's note: 'Allons enfants de la patrie, le jour de gloire est arrivé' ('Come, children of our country, the day of glory has arrived') is the first line of the *Marseillaise*. What they were actually singing was, 'Come, children of martyrdom, Blacks have lively days.'

day to come round when Sister Marie-France gave dictation, for he was an excellent speller. There was once a piece by Marcel Proust that had been particularly challenging, but in the end he managed to sort out the agreement of the reflexive verbs. Sister Marie-France's generosity was boundless: every mistake was rewarded with a swipe on the head with a wooden ruler.

'Now you, Zoë,' fired the Sister. 'How do you spell "Europeans"?'

'Like it's said, Sister – "Youro-peyans".'

'You bunch of heathen illiterates! You ignoramuses!'

Her eyes flashed and fury punctuated her shouts with hearty cracks of the ruler. All the pupils were shaking in their shoes. Zoë fought to hold back her tears of disappointment, while the Sisters' son laughed at his teacher's furious outbursts.

'As for you, you impertinent boy,' seethed Sister Marie-France, glaring at him, 'don't laugh at your friends! As a penance you will say the rosary three times while you reflect upon the painful mysteries of Our Lord Jesus Christ.'

'Can I say my rosary tomorrow, Friday, after Confession?'

'You will say it tonight! Don't haggle with me! This isn't Douala market, and we're not under the palaver tree.'

Douo-Papus had suffered countless torments at the hands of his teachers. It wasn't that he was naughty. He just liked to laugh at his friends. In class, the slightest misdemeanour was a punishable offence. He had been made to memorise the Latin and Greek dictionaries fifteen pages at a time. But Douo-Papus liked his teachers and was always willing to prove it. Some even wondered if he didn't try to get punished on purpose. They used to say of him that he was 'as wise as a pope'.

It was said that Father Gaspard had been touched by God's grace while he was still a legionnaire, which was why he'd joined the Order of the Missionaries of the Holy Spirit. He was also said, or so legend had it, to be ambitious, erudite, a shrewd judge of the human spirit, a builder. His discourses were full of recollections. And while he never doubted they were his own, there was something strange about them. He had witnessed the worst. Alone one night, spitting fragments of steel, with only an axe and a bowl of light, he tackled a group of weary warriors. He was a legionnaire. To a child of eleven, this could only mean the Legion of Mary who, like necromancers, could raise the dead, who could bring ghosts to life and who defended those who carried the cross in the fight against the infidel. Nothing could stand in the way of anyone who'd been dealt destiny's cards.

Douo-Papus could picture Father Gaspard in a white cassock, feet shod in monks' sandals, conquering invisible enemies. He could see him descending into hell, making his way through the ultimate darkness only to reappear as the glorious bringer of divine light. Extraordinary blood coursed through his veins. He was Saint Anthony, the thief of light who embraced the night; Orpheus, prising open the abyss. Comforting with his song the inconsolable distance, he defied the Kingdom of the Shades. Surrounded by the invisible, he cast out the light.

Halfway between heaven and earth, the still reflection of Father Gaspard was, to Douo-Papus, like a father's protective presence. He was just as capable of picturing the brightness of a papaya in bloom, its glossy, puckered fruits like the heavens, with, at the top, a turquoise gorge, a blossoming of stars sucked, it seemed, from fragile green to pure gold by the tropical heat. Douo-Papus walked in Father Gaspard's shadow. In the dark, he could intuit the black-white grain of the mangrove and the pale rings of the guava. When they went out hunting, his eye would sometimes glimpse the illuminated fragments of a cobbled-together stall. From almost one end to the other, the water frayed and receded. Kingfishers called to their mothers; the slow processions of sparrows spread their clouds peppered with stars westward. Douo-Papus had returned to primitive times, to a universe ocellated with light and darkness, to a unified landscape where the child was returned to his mother's bosom. He was afraid of nothing now. The Father's gaze watched over him. His origins had been returned to him.

Douo-Papus was moved, as much by the austerity of his years in the convent, as by the memory of Father Gaspard performing Schubert's *Winter's Journey*. Never before had he heard anything like it. He could picture again the village at the dawning of his life, the women in their floating *kabas*, hoeing the earth. He could hear the birds, drip by endless drip, calling to one another, recreating their sonorous structures in the splintering night. It was nothing like the jubilant din of tom-toms or the syncopated chant of balaphons.

When Father Gaspard played the *Stabat Mater*, Douo-Papus wondered what unknown memory was stirred, which only strengthened his resolve to experience winter, to visit the holy cities that other nations, those closer to the living God, had built.

It was necessary, however, for his dark and desolate side to disintegrate and dissolve into a single double culture. Swallowed up by his double memory, the child, having chosen to be absent, had lived without possessions. Doubly erased, he had lost his name. The sky was the mirror in which he searched for his face without being able to find it. Constantly falling apart, he continued to live the contented absence of one who wrote his name only to fade away.

▼

Douo-Papus was well read, too well read for his age. At twelve, he could analyse the mores of Molière's Italian farce. At thirteen, he could work out whether the clash of weapons was the result of a conflict of honour or passion. Without ever having read Shakespeare, he knew Shakespearean themes were to be found in Césaire's *Tempest*. But he'd never read the books children of his age might have read. He'd not heard of Robert Louis Stevenson, Jules Verne or Alexander Dumas. He was a child who had sought refuge deep in the heart of literature. Having read books he hadn't always understood, he'd travelled the length and breadth of foreign lands, discovered forbidden cities and devastated landscapes, and penetrated the breath of the world.

A nostalgic scribe, he religiously reproduced the strange mix of French and vernacular, amazed that people said *misérer* (meaning to eke out a wretched existence), *fréquenter* (meaning to go to school), *cadeauter* (meaning to give a present) and *préparer* (meaning to cook). The nuns would often find him rapt in the analysis of these weird expressions. Douo-Papus loved the austere thrill language gave him, the smooth, scintillating night of words that meant the world was but a whisper away.

In his convent bedroom at night, Douo-Papus would once again see himself nestled against his mother's burgeoning, blossoming breasts. He'd find himself in a state of pure ecstasy. The powerful and larger-than-life image he had of his mother, of the day she was so cruelly taken from him, was that of an overwhelmingly glorious, ghostly presence. He was like the child in Vladimir's *The Mother of God* who instinctively pressed his cheek against the Virgin's grief-stricken face. With a comforting caress he eased the suffering yet to come. Founder of a new mystery, Douo-Papus had created a symbology that put him beyond everyone's reach. When, lost in the contemplation of the mystery of the mother, he communed with her through the sign of the cross. It was as though – his hand no louder than his voice – the cry he'd uttered at birth had choked him before it could burst out.

Such religious paintings as *St George Slaying the Dragon* or *Christ on the Mount of Olives* were very different from the secular paintings Douo-Papus came across in the convent library. Having developed a passion for painting, he revelled in the mastery of a work like Giovanni Bellini's *Woman at Her Toilet* whose shimmering nudity moved him to a spiritual musing on matter. The cloth draped around the woman barely concealed the flesh tints, the negative of flesh. Reflected in the mirror, her cumbersome headdress split her body in two and unveiled the light of an invisible flame. Reality, whose cold colours offset the baroque headgear, gradually emerged from the landscape, in the left of the painting. It looked as though the sky had been infused with the scents, the dreams and yearnings of he who was studying it.

Hope and hunger merged whenever

Douo-Papus contemplated François Boucher's *Diana Emerging from Her Bath*. Mystery and rage were appeased by the epic fable that told the story of the gods. Every hue could be found in the skin's extraordinary candour. And in a painting like Botticelli's *Birth of Venus*, Eros was spiritualised. To Douo-Papus it was the apparition of the white Virgin. He was Actaeon, hidden in the bushes, glimpsing the forbidden. Anxious to protect her virginity, Diana might have been about to turn him into a stag, condemned to be killed by his own hounds. But the innocent union the child – a prey to his own desires – celebrated with Diana the huntress, won him the purple of real royalty.

While it was probably in his nature to fall back on his imagination, the real driving force was the actuality of monastic life, confined as he was to the school and convent walls which he found suffocating. Although he knew he was ill-equipped for life, he longed to embrace it. And while passion, sensuality and hunger made him yearn to live life to the full, he was prevented from doing so by the deepening fissure, the void inside him that drove him further into his imaginary world.

How many times had he promised himself he would stop being sucked in by his imagination, that he would never again embrace ghosts, but only people made of flesh and blood, the living reality he craved! That is how he came to fall in love with a young woman he'd glimpsed down by Lake Bonabéri. Wave upon delightful wave of dreams and yearnings, crystallised in blue reflections, flooded through him. But he was afraid that in the eyes of this older woman, he was nothing but a mere child. His whole life had sought refuge in a tyrannical vision that seemed to be secretly illuminated and glowing with a poignant aura that was all he could identify with – he had become nothing but a great void around a tiny unforgettable point.

If the unmistakable intensity of his yearnings suddenly filled Douo-Papus with fear, it was because he thought they might stand in the way of his seizing the things of this world that he continued to want to hold.

▼

The French language – which was neither his nor his mother's tongue – did,
however, more thoroughly than any
idiolect would have done, plough the
patient furrow of words. Never had he
had a gift like this adopted language of
his, to which he constantly returned
like one obsessed with its syntax and
secrets, haunted by Daudet's light-
filled Provence, by the social struggles
of Zola's Paris and the vitality of La
Fontaine's *Fables*. He might as well
have attempted to reproduce the
cricket's chirring in the night, the sea's
cold breath, the nuns' redundant out-
pourings, the hummingbird's strange
poetry, the landscape, and the light and
voices of childhood. Later he would
understand that this same silence could
be heard in Flaubert's dreamy, wind-
ing, crepuscular and wistful phrasing,
and with heady precision, in the miracle of languages that single-handedly
reawakened the vanity of being born.

While some sought to banish the
world by taking up religion, he turned
in on himself and, in a state of static

ecstasy, tamed words. In the blue of the sky he examined the fragments of a memory that was never his, but which offered him vague babblings, the dream of origins forever lost and the exquisite thrill of new foundations.

Moreover French was the all too fleeting mirror, the orphan tongue into which he was born.

That he didn't have a mother tongue made him dream. Of the mysterious sound structures there was only ever a sudden yearning or insane longing that trotted out deep in his heart the great French language that reverberated from Montaigne to Julien Gracq. The contemptible mumble of native languages had revealed to him the silence of writing, the impossible relationship with the other, the fear of conflict.

Much later, he understood that writing was connected to the pleasures of the mouth, and saw how it was part of a relatively untouched carnal land, created in the seduction of the pleasures of the flesh, a brutal reminder of his other identity. Each day the writer invents both the mother and the son.

▼

Paris

I never imagined just how moving I, Douo-Papus at the age of fourteen, would find the day I arrived in Paris. It was seven in the evening and in Africa it was already dark. Dazed and bewildered, I watched the night that wouldn't fall. Having left Roissy-Charles de Gaulle Airport, my eyes feasted on the magnificence and sophistication of the capital whose power, culture and beauty had been admired by so many Africans. From my taxi I saw flash past patrician residences, magnificent and beautifully proportioned palaces whose façades were adorned with mouldings and triumphal arches; cemeteries and riverbanks. My senses and thoughts were besieged by grandiose buildings, half-glimpsed parks, basilicas outlined against the sky, tarmac roads, and the Seine never far from sight, the combined splendour that stone and water bestowed on each other. I was speechless. Having admired the absolute perfection of it all, what was there left to look forward to? I had dreamed of this unfamiliar France; of rocking myself in dreams, in travels; but the reality was dazzling in its intensity.

I was to live with a spiritual community in rue Lhomond. I explored the huge labyrinthine building around which, again and again, I took slow repetitive walks in the hope of breaking my isolation. But no one spoke to me and I dared speak to no one.

After the initial bedazzlement, Paris can become somewhat boring to anyone who doesn't know the city. I wandered the streets for days on end in search of the treasures whose virtues had been lauded. But I found the melting pot of languages and cultures a complete maze. In the capital, differences become blurred, and apart perhaps from a few Senegalese, illegal street-traders and refuse collectors with whom I could identify, all the passers-by were white.

Paris smokes. And the smells got to my throat. A blanket of grey hung over the city. A hazy, sooty sky blocked out the horizon. It was as though the land-scape of exile was drenched in a pale light that didn't so much plunge one into mourning, but rather, slowly accli-matised one to absence.

Every day I walked around Paris. The walls of old buildings towered high above me, their round arches crowned with a bull's eye whose name alone gave me the unpleasant sensation that I was being watched. As I made my way, I was surprised to see the light from an invisible sun. The tangle of thoroughfares and tree-lined streets was the absolute opposite of the forest, more delicious, more irritating than it would have been in a tropical climate, for it was constantly moving, engulfed, saturated, then instantly distorted by the mass of vehicles striating with metallic flashes and unfriendly vibra-tions the hazy reds of sunset.

Walking along the boulevards and striding down the streets stirred mem-ories of a great, mutable joy. It was like walking through the dense forest. I searched in vain for Father Gaspard's gaze. But no such gaze watched over me.

And why were all these passers-by in such a hurry? And while I'd been affected by the sight of the endless palavers in Douala and Bonabéri, it wasn't so much because I could see my fellow countrymen sheltering from the tremors and wrath of the weather, but because witnessing the indolence in which Africa basked gave me a sense of familiarity.

How could I have liked the noise and bustle of Paris life when it was the sight of this rejection of time that thrilled me the most?

Maybe it was only ever me and my inner emotion that I had loved since childhood, on hearing the enchanted voice in my blood and my throat, whose echo was returned by the nuns, imbued always with the same sensitivity.

▼

Like all Africans, I had dreamed about winter. Maybe I even cherished the idea that my skin might eventually turn the colour of snow. My greatest wish was to be brown not black, which resulted in my being haunted by the strangest of allegories, that of Winter. Exemplary, shining Winter, redeemer of the soul and bringer of whiteness. To a soul that yearned for virginity and opulence, that was besotted with ancient voyages and ruins, this was to pitch uncontrollably into dream. I was in no doubt that, thanks to winter, white people had been given a natural wealth of endless holidays. Only in Europe could the happy union of idleness and comfort, the promise and hope of an elsewhere be found sheltering in the shade of its famous cities, where blessed harmony opens up vast perspectives to the imagination.

Condensation of humours in the sky, could snow not be some kind of appeasement or even of happiness? A breeze dropped onto the town, it was hardened then sterilised – but where did it come from? Icy wind, Siberian cold, sterile brutality, cruel pincers that gripped me tighter than any others. He who has travelled the northern deserts knows how resilient the soul can be. I thought I would die of cold. Crushed by the deadly desolation of these distant lands, I renounced the illusion of immortality on which the African imagination feeds.

Paralysed, the earth explodes, is covered with a tracery of cracks, chilblains, scratches, scars, cuts, a complex infinity of marks to be deciphered. For the earth to at last become legible snow is required; only that petrified memory can erase, beneath its uniform mantel, all traces of a strange harshness. It is as though the world has changed into a vast vanity that condemns snow to dissolve into the dullness of mud. What must one have committed to deserve such dereliction? All that is left is a long solitary meditation from which, transformed, one wakes to the enduring breath of the world.

In times of distress, when the invisible is lost, the beauty of snow remains. It falls, immaculate, earth and sky merge, and the hushed countryside freezes over as the huge tumbrel of desolation passes by. Having shuffled the heavy clouds, the plain unfolds the lost and unanticipated whiteness of dazzling glades. Translucent and deep, the snow has abandoned greatness to cart its ashes and carry its promises. Meadows and woods, hedges and trees, hills and rivers, so many elements are locked into the sky's adventure.

The surrounding earth becomes waterlogged; whitish halos stagnate in fields whose endless dreary banality can be felt stretching as far as the horizon. The Île-de-France is steeped in a deep and silent mystery – light and shade lie in each other or gradually drift apart – this is the miracle that turns it into a garden of discovery. Beyond the heaviness of the here-and-now towards an elsewhere, winter landscapes are a frozen temptation to the soul. While they were no cure for melancholy, they

at least reconciled me to myself,
soothed and nourished me. That in my
land of exile, snow should so easily
lend itself to dream, was enough to satisfy me.

▼

For a long time, as though my mother still loved me, as though she had never abandoned me, as though her breath were mingled with my own, I surrendered to the illusion of memory, to its magic in the dimple of light that made my orphan roots quiver. This constant harking back, I never got over it. I'd fall asleep with my memories, snug in my images of childhood and my earliest games with my mother. I could no longer differentiate nostalgia from the only time in my life I was completely happy, content to live in the here-and-now.

But where was my truth now? Drowned in the bluish translucence of my mother's milk or hidden in the touching faces, for ever and ever diffracted, that appeared suddenly in the torrent of memories? The day I first ate snails, I felt again the same fleeting emotion kindled by light, felt the same delight as when, one muggy night during the dry season in Douala, I munched an enormous desert locust, grilled on a hurricane lamp. It was the same amazing experience each time I recalled it.

For hours I wouldn't move, feeling deep within me territories reclaimed from oblivion, from which sudden shafts of memories would appear out of the blue to besiege and almost choke me. So the day I pushed open the door of St Saviour's Church, my whole childhood flooded back, intact, down to the sound of my sandals on the flagstones, the candlelight in the side aisles, the mystery of the tabernacle, the mingled scent of incense and wax, the strange aroma that took me back to another time. It was as if – coexisting with the nuns' heavy wimples, the fabric of their old-fashioned habits, the actual smell of monastic life – all I had to do was get a whiff of it for the memory to return, unaltered.

I was unwittingly subjected to a most important ceremony. There I was watching over the sacred, breathing the biting air. The faint echo of my feet on the flagstones was barely audible. Everything shifted to another dimension – silence, time, distance. It seemed to me that I had left the world behind and that I was moving through the dark to enter a deep, dense solitude. I spoke softly. A young, still immature light dripped from the tabernacle. Night's embrace took me back to my origins. My mind was empty, so completely absorbed was I in the Presence that was filling me with light. The unreal, magical sensation lifted me heavenwards. How was I to address the austere bliss carved in the measured pulsing of the light? The candle went out. A crow fled the elder. There might have been the creaking of a worm-eaten church door.

All the women, all the nuns had loved me with giddy adoration as the son they had never had. I had suckled in pain until I was two. And yet, no feeling was more rooted in me than that of absence because I had been a child sated with my mother; I had lived at the sharp end of excess and excesses, and become a being of memory.

As a child, I might well have prayed to God to punish my mother, indeed, to take her life, secretly hoping He wouldn't answer my prayer. Deep in my heart I wished it whenever the nuns upset me. And so, when I was at my angriest, the resentment I felt for my mother was physical, and I'd ask God to deprive her forever of children. She had to be punished for having deserted me.

I'd shout, 'Oh! How happy I'd be if you couldn't have any more children! Then you'd be sorry you abandoned me!' But having knotted a creeper and wanted her dead, I'd repent and days later I'd still be filled with remorse.

Numb, I didn't know what to focus on; it seemed that time had swept everything away, past happiness, the first five years spent with my mother, and all hope – however pathetic, however strong, of ever making up for the absence of a mother's love that revived the hurt inside me.

The thwarted, mutilated lives of these two individuals, mother and son, both of them prevented, in part the one by the other – and the one *because* of the other – from finding fulfilment. Love itself mutilated by their deadly vocation for sacrifice. All that remained between them was the shadow of God.

▼

That morning, the games I used to play as a child came back to me; shadow puppets, hopscotch that led straight to heaven, five players competing for four corners, hide and seek, leapfrog, draughts, ludo, cards, catapult, ball games with friends, cars made out of sardine tins and bamboo that were such good imitations of the big ones that I'd drift into a daydream, and marbles – those beautiful, delicately banded marbles I hardly dared play with, a whole area of my imaginary empire, momentarily basking in the banished light.

A sense of shame at the dreadful puns that circulated in rue Lhomond brought me back to reality. The cheap word games – 'droppings from the flying spirit' ('Saul, Saul, why persecutest thou me? Why piercest thou me queue[2]?') – proved only too well, despite my indignation, just how sensitive I was to unbridled flights of fancy and weird jokes, and if I refrained from

[2] The French word used is 'cul' meaning 'arse'.

giving in to this somewhat ambiguous fascination, it was only because I found this type of humour blasphemous. To me the sanctity of language, which had at all costs to be preserved, was in danger of being undermined by the sacrilege and that, once sullied, once blasphemed, the words might become obsolete, having forever relinquished their duty to mystery and lost the spark with which they celebrate their union with language.

Not one of these word games wasn't dubious. I was always monitoring myself for improper associations. And if I was so fond of board games, maybe it was because the word itself was symptomatic of my own boredom. How often did I say that? Did I do it to hurt myself, to convince myself, to intensify the pain I felt in the very flesh of language; that unforgettable, insurmountable wound that always prevented me from blending with the crowd, from enshrouding myself in my exile?

These opportune coincidences became

more sporadic and more fleeting. In the end absence prevailed and dismantled language. There was nothing left; even the bright flashes that still surfaced a while ago had vanished. I was constantly confronted with the image of a blasted language, and this image blocked out all others, including the precarious miracles to which I still clung, the oracular flashes that had snatched me from exile.

▼

The interrogation going on inside my head was unremitting. Alarmed, I began to wonder if I hadn't imagined the whole thing – not my first encounter with the sacred in the convent oratory, but the dizzying flight to a life more imagined than real. Swept away by the breath of God, I had wanted to be one with the happy icon of eastern Christians, depicting the Virgin and Child.

And it was the same images that returned during my long solitary walk from St Saviour's when, to my surprise, I came across a crowd gathered in the square. What a surprise, what a shock, and what a disappointment to learn that it was a spontaneous demonstration in support of the homeless. Same obsessions in Paris as in Yaoundé then, and once again I could picture the Sunday market outside the Cathedral of Notre Dame.

In the tentative light of dawn, long before the sun's reflections had dissolved, women would set out from the furthest outskirts, baskets of miscellaneous items or bundles of cloth balanced on their heads. Pre-empting the sultriness of the dry season, they spread their raffia mats, where red and yellow peppers, yams, sweet potatoes and whatever fruit was in season bloomed. Demands for the best spots followed by the raucous reproaches of irate shrews battling it out, then voices fusing, diffusing, finding their rhythm, becoming regular, harmonious, melodic – the stallholders were ready. The heavy aroma of braised beef, whiffs of rancid fat and potted lamb, the stale smell of millet flour and mashed banana fritters encapsulated the very notion of an opulence that had carried into the distance the effluvium of its merits. At this, a time of the great affluence, there were young people in the streets, fresh out of university, living on the fringes of a society unable to find them a job, illegally selling articles stolen from stalls. The more ingenious ones became street entertainers and worked on developing their acrobatic and balancing skills. Heads spinning from laughing at the comedians' jokes and their clever though predictable digs at politicians, the onlookers thoroughly enjoyed watching the jugglers.

They vied with one another – as their bodies jerked violently, their aching limbs juddered and their heads shook all over the place – to see whose joints would crack the most and the loudest. The tightrope walkers clattered rhythmically to the beat of drums and clapping. The roar from the crowd grew louder, urging the victor on to more daring displays of prowess. But there were those who booed, arguing that he had exploited a weakness that meant he could dislocate his hip at will.

A dozen little old men in the crowd, all very chipper and full of beans, up from some village buried in the countryside, were burping loudly, having made the most of what the market had to offer. These indecorous eructations upset their neighbours who waved their hands in the air in disgust. The same little men made their way to the farters' club where, greedy and grasping, and high on competitive spirit, they were determined to put on a lengthy show so as to do justice to the food they had guzzled. The day before they had cleansed their stomachs of all impurities then taken equal portions of parsley, lemon balm and mint. The wiliest had chosen red kidney beans and green apples to encourage gaseous emissions. Leaning forwards, hands on knees, they took a deep breath, held it, squeezed their muscles, arched their backs, shut their mouths, puffed out their cheeks and finally forced out a magnificent blast.

Vile smells were prohibited. A nose patrolled and showed its worth by designating the one the spectators should reward with their loose change. The winner had discharged a unique and particularly pleasurable perfume that we presumed he alone could produce. It was a new variety; the only one able to create a heavenly and spiritual universe that would cleanse the world of mediocrity and foulness. What was it then that had provided the proof of this bliss – a bliss that banished reality?

Every market has its own individual buried emotions. Lingering over La Briqueterie market, like the smell of civet or ambergris, there was a strong, exceedingly sensual, musky scent that encapsulated the heady charms of Hausa women. Further away, in the main market, rough, wrinkled vanilla pods released their bittersweet fragrance into the delicate and exquisite haze of cinnamon. Finally, in Etoudi market, the combined scent of aniseed, ginger, nutmeg, paprika and saffron evoked a far-off, lost, near-extinct world, an aromatic forest. Such is Yaoundé, shimmering with complicated olfactory structures, a veritable museum of memories, a synaesthesia of voluptuousness, essential, silent and still, where – when the sky enfolds its seven hills – all boundaries are lost.

▼

Like an obsession almost, the memory came back of my first French lessons with Sister Capitolina who – always patient, always admirable – would squeeze my shoulder every time I failed to pronounce the letter 'r' ('The tewible Pawis plague.' 'No! The terrible Paris plague.'). Strange regress to childhood, but these mistakes were as firmly rooted as my favourite poem or the hackneyed refrain I sometimes found myself humming.

Memory's tumbrel had probably neither cleansed nor absolved me of the lingering odours of sacrilege and blasphemy. Pressed against Sister Capitolina, I'd wait for her to correct my mistakes with prepositions with that habit the nuns had of tweaking a cheek whenever a pupil broke the rules of grammar. In the dwindling afternoon, I was happy. Vying with the quality of this happiness, as well as the stirrings of desire and quieting of language, were minute details that galvanised the magic of memory. It was as though my happiness depended on memory and me remaining at odds, strangers to one another, in the churning of blood and the terror of mutual rejection. But had the feeling of happiness, particularly when in the form of ecstasy, not always heralded disaster?

Sister Capitolina gave me a rosary made of coral beads from the banks of the River Wouri. To feel it next to my heart filled me with the same delight, the same imperceptible anguish as the nun's fleeting presence; it was as if a tiny, translucent sliver of coral had for all time touched my heart. These blissful moments were more important to me than any others, for the remembering of them crystallised the fragments of my exile. There are those objects, which – like awe in the presence of a loved one – reopen a wound, take a person to a higher level of nakedness and then consecrate and expand him. As though I had been stabbed by beauty, I remained frozen, like a dead pharaoh, listening for the silence into which the blue gaze of a Madonna and Child had gradually faded.

Sitting outside the Café Flore I'd watch the passers-by. Many were those who sported Bermuda shorts. I presumed they were as poor as the coastal inhabitants who had but one pair of trousers between three. And there was me thinking you could pick money out of the gutter! And to think that some young Africans bankrupted themselves so they could strut around in the latest fashions, cherishing the illusion they were living like Parisians.

I did have incredible experiences like these back home, though not so often, and I remember jumping for joy whenever I caught sight of the hibiscus flowers in full bloom against the convent wall just before they fell apart. In Douala too, even in Douala! It was the almost childish thrill I got from watching the locust die on the hurricane lamp, the whimsical flight of dragonflies as they settled, as though out of breath, on a flower, their veined wings sparkling in the sun. The burn of anamnesis and the inexplicable damage it wreaked only served to increase my pain and bewilderment; I didn't need to see the old nun limping around the convent gardens or Father Gaspard's solitary silhouette to be reminded of my exile.

On that December morning I didn't feel much like working, so I decided to go for a walk. The streets were so crowded that with each step I took I felt I was putting my life at risk. Dark, grey-edged clouds soon covered the sky. The first drops of rain made me think of the idleness I had forfeited. Children in Africa are let off school when it rains. No such freedom in France, not even a reprieve – it's life imprisonment from September to July. I did, however, bring back from this walk some fairly unusual, if not crazy impressions. It was as if I'd been fleeing as well as seeking them in order to feed my adolescent dreams.

The streets were so crowded that I had the feeling there was something dreadful at the side of the road and in amongst the tightly packed cars. It was like a slow suffocation created in part by exhaust fumes. The traffic bothered me because it brought to the surface half-buried recollections of days spent wandering the forest with Father Gaspard. The priest would leave the car at the entrance to the village. It was a poetic sight, the wind stirring the bracken, and he the white stain at the heart of the tall restless shafts that I could only just see but had to follow not to get lost.

I was hurrying along the streets, having turned back when the first sporadic hesitant drops of rain had begun to fall, when I had the distinct impression of a sprightly gait just ahead of me. I searched in vain for Father Gaspard's heavy silhouette so that I could enjoy the old feeling of intimacy the impression had brought me, and which I thought I could experience again, just for a second. What I probably wanted to hear was the Father reaffirming his faith in me by speaking the words I remembered: 'Come along, little mite. Don't worry, I'll clear a path.' Because that was what I secretly longed for.

I believed I'd never die in peace until I had painstakingly, almost lovingly described the Father's ritual, which he acted out whenever he went to visit the Pygmies in the equatorial forest. I wanted to describe every one of his gestures – the way he anointed his body with a potion to keep snakes and mosquitoes at bay. I'd hear the conversations in Pygmy, from which I felt excluded. I recalled the ritual dances celebrating the beheading of their enemies; the skulls, displayed like trophies, from which – revolted and fascinated – I couldn't tear my eyes; the little men stuffing their short-stemmed pipes with hemp. I thought I would never be free of these images.

Child that I was, it never occurred to me that my mother might have missed *me*. Shame, stupor, exile, bewilderment, I felt them all the moment I left Douala for Paris. At mealtimes in rue Lhomond, I felt foreign, isolated. Those entering the priesthood would talk, laugh and encourage me to eat, but to me it seemed that a path was forever closing behind me. Had I not been cast out of paradise and plunged into another world? Henceforth I would remain suspended between the old universe, the only true one, to which I would never return, and the new world which rejected me as much as I rejected it. Indeed, for a long time I suffered the pain of having no family, no tribe, no home and no homeland. I was alone, without roots.

Night after night I dreaded going to bed in a strange room, full of strangers. Although there was nothing about the room that was frightening, I was afraid I might wet the bed or be unable to sleep. As it happened I couldn't sleep. I was scared that if I did, the young bed-wetter's dreams would return. And yet all I wanted was to sleep, to find inner peace, to end the anguish and never again reawaken my old ghosts. To calm myself down, I'd pray, recite Siméon's *Nunc dimittis* in the belief that prayer could help, that God – if I addressed Him directly – would intervene personally and bring me sleep. Head buried under the sheets, engrossed in the prayers I was mouthing, my misery did not subside. Through the long night, I'd hear the hours strike. And each time the tenor bell sounded so my anguish grew. I was driven to despair when I realised what time it was, that two, three hours had passed and that I was still not asleep, that I would still be awake at dawn.

▼

At fifteen the person I most admired was Father Marie-Pâques. He was the one who represented the ultimate image to which I desperately aspired. In his sermons, which I attended each week, it wasn't simply his intelligence, so sharp, so great, so superior to mine, that fascinated me, but the actual words, the unique tone, the profound breath of a human being. What I loved were the harmonics his words triggered in me, which seldom bore any relation to the biblical text he was analysing. Not only were his ideas original, rich and profound, but also often miraculous. Where there might have been confusion he had the ability to inspire wonder. I wanted to be like him, able to talk for hours on any verse, able to instantly grasp the beauty or the uniqueness of a parable, able to explain how to behave, what pitfalls to avoid, all the lessons of life that I, Douo-Papus, still did not know.

This image of Father Marie-Pâques towering over me during Mass as I listened with ever-increasing fervour –

how could I not have found it sublime, how could I not have been filled with quasi-religious admiration for him? And how could I have known that the image Father Marie-Pâques projected of himself was, unbeknown to me, not his real face, not a true reflection of who he was, but rather the image of the person I wanted to be? The image was permanently engraved in me however, with the result that I felt weak, diminished.

For years the image I had of Father Marie-Pâques was that of a great, a noble being. Although the model was unachievable, to me it was the only one worth emulating. In the final analysis I wanted *to be* Father Marie-Pâques – not the man himself but the saint who wore his face. For the first time in my life I developed a guilty conscience, an insidious contempt born of shame, of remorse for not being him.

What I most admired in Father Marie-Pâques was the father he represented. As a child I'd been unable to look to my father to satisfy my need to have someone to admire; as a consequence I tried all the harder to find someone to fulfil that role, especially as my untapped capacity for admiration had been damaged by the affection heaped upon me by the nuns.

I probably nurtured a secret yearning for this law as well as an unwitting abhorrence for the long and paralysing liberty to which I saw myself reduced. For a long time Father Marie-Pâques's words were my law, a law to which I was only too ready to succumb since, in my eyes, the man who offered it was more of an example; was in fact *the example* I had never had. Admittedly I didn't think of Father Marie-Pâques as a father, but there was no doubting that he filled the place vacated by my father. Only much later did I understood that it was through God that I loved Father Marie-Pâques, and that He was the one I wanted to reach in the endless addresses that served as prayers.

For what preoccupied me was a longing, a concern for salvation. To me, as for many others, a life without loving, without worshipping God was empty, meaningless. In itself my life was nothing; only the Word, the praising of God could make it worthwhile – could, in a word, save it. The only thing of which I was sure was my vocation as a priest. And the only value I accepted was that of a secular world inhabited, illuminated, made meaningful and full only by the Word.

I sensed the first signs of God when I entered the convent. This secret yearning for transcendence, for this Other to give meaning to my sacrificed destiny, were sublimated by Father Marie-Pâques, proof in itself that the same fervour, the same yearning he so passionately inspired in me existed in him. Unbeknownst to him, Father Marie-Pâques had in a way replaced God, become God. What I had done was to project onto religion the whole of my strange and somewhat extreme view of the sacred.

In my dream, the door opened of its own accord; he came through it as slowly and proudly as if he had descended from heaven; the branches of the trees were bowed by a blast of wind; he trampled the dead flowers – and something extraordinary took place between Father Marie-Pâques's eyes and mine that raised me up for ever. Of course, nothing of the kind ever really happened.

Father Marie-Pâques didn't want me to be friends with anyone. He forced me into a gradually more total solitude, one to which he himself would have liked to devote himself. Nevertheless, I was in no doubt that Father Marie-Pâques saw me as a kind of spiritual son, the child he had never had, and I believed that he wanted to mould me in the image of the ideal person he was urging me to become.

I had never admired an individual, one I was close to, as much as I did Father Marie-Pâques – apart from Father Gaspard that is, whose mythical, almost imaginary personality I idolised. I had given my heart to Father Gaspard, in much the same way that others give themselves to God. With tears in my eyes, I thought of snow and the blue shade of a solitary sisal. Father Marie-Pâques I would remember with the same kind of devotion as that of believers devoted to the sublime and veiled image of their God.

▼

Was dawn breaking in me? If not, what was the source of the divided bitter joy, the feeling of incompleteness I felt every morning as I slid into prayer? I, who viewed the world without indifference. I, who was serious, tense, introspective, watching the candlelight for the unacceptable revelation. I wasn't aware of the destructive forces that had been at work in me since time immemorial – so much so that I'd spent my whole life battling against or trying to avoid them. As I must have wasted years and most of my energy on this futile, dubious struggle to preserve a wrecked happiness, how could this dreadful loss not have left me empty and vulnerable?

The call of God and the strange havoc it wreaked in me found the spark it needed to erupt and take me over completely.

My presence in this foreign city on the other side of the world, shut up in a tiny room where I worked alone, surprised me. I was naïve enough to believe that the voices urging me to perform my devotions were bringing me closer to God. I hardly dared raise my eyes, for it seemed to me that either I had glimpsed that which I had no wish to see, or that which above all else I wished to see. I could just as easily have rejoiced as wept. I rose to the warmth of the night, my mouth full of something sweet like death. On the brink of the darkest of raptures, unable to choose between the light revealed to me and the night that threatened me, daring to rouse the unbearable hidden spot within me, which I perhaps didn't want to know was there, I was sinking, drowning in lies. Shaken from top to toe, a crack appeared, the essential being was freed and it was as though glowing, glorious, indefatigable love, was constantly stirring in me!

But this feeling of intoxication, of unbridled joy existed only in me. I was filled with an aching relief, but I was also very weak.

This ghost, this child who was finding it so difficult to grow up, could not get over losing his mother, and his eyes brimmed with tears whenever he remembered the day she abandoned him, whenever he thought he'd die far from her, in an anonymous community of exiles. Could it be that he too was a stateless person, a useless fossil from an obsolete world? It was as if – although the piteous sacrifice of a life already dispossessed had distressed and attached me more firmly to my mother – the heartache of living the life of a recluse had revealed the sacred to me.

Since my arrival, I had experienced bouts of self-pity that were instantly submerged by a combination of pain, remorse, hatred and almost disgust. And with each day that passed, I found them increasingly more difficult to suppress; there were times when resentment ran me through like a sword. All that I had been, all that I had known, that had moulded me, was no more.

I wasn't even eighteen, yet I had outlived a dead world that had become engulfed in me. The dreams from which dangled scraps of the sacred had scarcely changed since I was a child. There was probably no more bitter, nor more tender bond than this forever vanished past, the recollections of a time, which, far from being a comfort to me, were in danger of reopening an ineffaceable wound. Blinded by tears when I turned to it, could it be that this was my vocation – to indulge in emotion, to withdraw, to become intoxicated on suffering, to have the same intense and absolute sense of being lost only to rediscover myself?

I don't know what forces of inertia had been at work in me since childhood, so much so that the whole of my youth was a struggle against this innate passivity. For years this vile, muddled conflict must have weakened me; so how was it then that the terrible cost didn't leave me lacking the wherewithal to face the future?

The day I met Clara, was the world, was I emptied in one fell swoop, absorbed by all that blue? Did we disappear when the lake receded so far we thought it would never return? Alive again, tormented by the image of the first time I met Clara on the beach in Bonabéri, I reconnected with the dark powers that had found a reason to completely overwhelm me.

While Clara denied ever having been to Bonabéri, I remembered the creamy sky that had formed a halo of blue around her and into which I was desperate to disappear. The soft streaks of sunlight on the lake, the water mirror burned into me, like an apparition of the Virgin in the evening light.

More precious than reality, I embellished my imaginary version of our meeting a little more each day, and fleshed out my recollection of how I had felt at the sight of a face cast against the stars.

I was overjoyed when Clara agreed to see me again. Was it Clara I loved or the headiness, the thrill and just as acute, just as exhilarating pain rekindled by the memory and mingled with misery at the realisation that in Clara there would always be a dark corner I was desperate to reach? But at the time, and for the first time, all I could feel was a kind of spiritually sensual joy, a happiness so great that it was transforming me, the little boy of flesh and bones, who was seemingly in pain.

If I was conjuring an image of a girl as beautiful, as radiant as Clara, it was to convince myself she wasn't for me and that she'd never be mine. However, this didn't stop me from doing everything I could to be loved by her. Tenderly, I'd describe the memory she didn't share but which moved her deeply. Eyes fixed on the turquoise veil high above, I was past wanting to describe the state of bliss I was in. At that precise moment, I was sure words were more alive, more mysterious, more real than the things they named and it seemed to me that I – the hero of my own tale and of a love yet to come – was invested with the same sacredness I had bestowed on them.

Leaving the hostel in rue Lhomond, I held Clara's hand. I was instantly overcome by a stupid bout of shyness; I was the awkward child again who, since I'd known Sister Capitolina, I thought I had left behind. I hadn't been able to resist putting my hand in hers, bringing it closer to me, clasping the fragile palm against me and, tightening my grip, feeling her heart beat. Clara wore her hair in a bun; I was enchanted by the haughty look it gave her. When Clara leaned forward slightly, I could see two hairpins glide over her nape; it inspired me with a childish desire to bend over her neck and tidy her hair. It was a desire not unlike my yearning to nestle against my mother's breasts, to return the embraces of which I'd never had enough.

But Clara was drifting away and I became obsessed by grief. I recalled Job's plaintive cries, for in my opinion he was the one who, better than anyone else, expressed the feeling of deprivation left me by my thwarted love. If I continued, with a mounting sense of inevitability, to reflect on my dead love, it was to go to the limits of my disgust so as to use it up. Though I dreaded it, I hoped to destroy once and for all the sacred aura surrounding my passion, to annihilate even the yearning for the radiant Clara who had never been mine.

I was unable to cut myself off from those I had once loved; delaying the moment I would forget them for ever. Just as I never forgot my walks with Father Gaspard, my lessons with Sister Capitolina, not to mention my ambiguous fascination with Father Marie-Pâques. There were times when

I allowed my love for Clara, my disappointment to return. My problematical passion for memory confirmed the terror that overwhelmed me, and from which I had hoped in vain and without really believing it, Clara would save me.

▼

Letters from Douala always fuelled my sense of isolation. One day a letter from Sister Capitolina arrived, informing me that Father Gaspard was dead. From which painful, hidden part of me, probably dating from the time I entered the convent, came that sense of guilt – that I had failed the only father I ever had? And yet I myself had suffered from the physical withholding of his affection, from his brusqueness and dispassionate attitude towards me.

My need to torment myself must have been great. Or was it that the memory I'd kept of the last time I'd seen the Father had somehow become so distorted it was impossible to recognise? All that was left me of Father Gaspard was – nothing – no trace, scarcely a memory, his grey hair tumbling onto his forehead, his infinitely weary expression, a mournful look, no more than that; his scattered bones, the funeral I wouldn't attend, the feeling that I, Douo-Papus, was alone in the world.

What was it that was eating away at

me during those years in exile? Was it the world, myself, my childish brooding over my happy early years, the shadow I continued to drag around, to trip over, from which only death could free me, the insatiable paternity that constantly revived me, tormented me as though it were joined to this desolate place, to my misery, to my infrangible solitude.

Douala. All those years in the convent, Father Gaspard had been aware of my hurt, of my suffering. All those years – and all those painful flashes of joy, that one rainy season. The poignant apparition of a much-loved silhouette between two papayas, one day out hunting. The precarious miracles to which I clung. Such inner turmoil! Once stirred, other memories, always the same, surfaced – my birth in the blue shade of a solitary sisal, the enchantment of my early childhood, diffracted images of my mother, myself, already in exile at the heart of my homeland.

That last rainy season in Douala, the

light had already gone from Father Gaspard's face; he knew it would soon be time to leave. I studied him for a long time. He had grown so old, so tired, so thin – his mind was already elsewhere. Confronted by the body that would soon be gone, I suddenly found myself imagining the young man he had once been, as brave a legionnaire as ever there was. I wasn't in the least bit embarrassed by or ashamed of my fantasy. Death's mask had always been visible on the faces of those I had loved. *Douala*. Squally showers and gusts of wind … in the cemetery behind Bonapriso Church, a rectangular hole awaits. It isn't a farewell as such, more the tangible outrage of absence. What could still matter to the crowd in the blue of mourning as paradise is preached – the sudden tremor, the searing pain? The silence. The time for ghosts to return, for destiny to call, that's what I was waiting for.

The light in my life, its glow, all the faces I had loved – how they filled me with nostalgia – a nostalgia that held me back, that tortured me. It was a hope, a yearning for a different unattainable life elsewhere; and what was so cruel was that it was hell-bent on loudly reminding me of my lost paradise, leaving me to brood over my anguish and the pain of dispossession. Blinded, stunned by the sometimes barely veiled, barely fractured happiness my meeting with Father Marie-Pâques and my love for Clara had brought me, I stumbled along destiny's dark path, never imagining that one day the abyss would come rushing back, and that *that* from which I was separated, would send me straight back to feeling empty and non-existent.

Ghosts, that's what the people I'd loved had become, fleeting shadows to whom I could not return for fear of losing them again. Their fixed gaze lived on only in me. Inert, obsessed by my own privation, I was right to believe I'd never been able to do anything but contemplate imperfect images of people I'd loved too much.

This morbid compulsion already existed, predating the causes of identifiable suffering, revealing the first hurt, the loss of a mother's love, which my adolescent passions had tried hard to conceal, to banish. But though privation might – by donning a mask – have changed its name, it was nonetheless still sorrow. Some sources of grief are inexhaustible.

Had childhood not eluded me from the start, had it not remained so alien, I might never have been bewitched by it; might never have had to keep returning to it. My impenetrable, inaccessible childhood, made still more bitter by exile, I had tried in vain to access, but each attempt left me more vulnerable.

How had hell reached into far-flung imaginations? For it was right here, in my unlikely country of exile. And Lucifer twisted his lips into a sardonic smile. Trudging through the mud, I rummaged behind the vast fog of memory for the repetitive echo of the locust's song, the impish grin of a new-born baby, the sadness of abandoned objects. Hell was *in* me, in all the memories that engulfed and bore me away, and which, instead of rejecting, I continued desperately to revive, through mesmerising images that tore me asunder, that tormented me, and all the while entreated me.

▼

My memory was so active it needed no prompting. But the day I lost the rosary made of coral beads from the banks of the River Wouri, that Sister Capitolina had given me to remember her by, I felt more alone than ever. I had tried to recapture the oppressive mugginess of Douala, childhood images that always filled the perfect and loving child I had been, with the same sense of awe – bush fires raging wildly, the verdant forest with its blue-green glints, ochreous expanses that stretched to the sea, the sun pealing out in a sky grown larger each day, whose blue wouldn't fade, the hard resilient brightness of boatmen casting off, the everyday, inexhaustible, real-life paradise I would recall with emotion. Then the sky would tilt towards a congealed light that would become increasingly more oppressive. Only the presence of the trees that hid the spirits of the forest brought me peace. Their slow lives, their quiet retreat inspired me to dream. I loved their green, the thrust of their branches, all that strength reaching for the sky, and the souls of the ancestors watching over me. My love of my country, intact; my longing, intact.

Maybe I had to experience heartache, and to grieve. Despite the new experiences, despite the people I'd met, the disappointments and joys that breathed life into me, and which death might anchor more firmly in me, the impenetrable permanence of my passion and my long painful attachment remained. How could I continue to believe that I could only be faithful to the ravaged landscapes I'd been deprived of, that there was nothing that hadn't come from them; and how could I have thought about anything else since in the dream that had become my life, I lived only there, haunted by the delicacy of the forest's silence, by the familiar scent of drenched coconut palms, by the magic held in the bluish reflection of the night sky, haunted by all the beauty that clung to me? My lost paradise, I had searched for it in brambles, in undergrowth, in fragile glades muffled in light, in the shadowy fog of exile, among ruins and overturned graves. And at last I had found it, my infinite homeland. It was there, exposed, ripped open inside me, and I would never leave it again.

Other BlackAmber titles:

Ma
    Gaston-Paul Effa

Ancestors
    Paul Crooks

Nothing But The Truth
    Mark Wray

Paddy Indian
    Cauvery Madhavan

Ordinary Lives
– Extraordinary Women
    Joan Blaney

The Holy Woman
    Qaisra Shahraz

What Goes Around
    Sylvester Young

Brixton Rock
    Alex Wheatle

One Bright Child
    Patricia Cumper